LOSING HIS COOL . . .

Dave, sensing the opportunity for a fast break, went streaking toward the Bulls' basket. The always alert Derek hit him with a one-hand baseball-style outlet pass. Dave saw just one olive-and-red Wildcats jersey between him and the basket. Jason Fox, anticipating the break, had hustled back on defense and stationed himself at the foul line.

Dave knew he could easily pass off to either Brian or Derek to beat the lone defender and score the go-ahead hoop. But he was still fuming over Fox's wise remarks at the start of the game.

Picking up steam as he approached the foul line, he rammed hard into Fox with his body. Dave used his left palm to straight-arm the huskier boy in the face—and still managed to get the layup off with his right hand.

It went in!

"No basket!" Mr. Sparks shouted.

Don't miss any of the books in

—a slammin', jammin', in-your-face action series
from Bantam Books!

#1 Crashing the Boards

#2 In Your Face!

#3 Trash Talk

#4 Monster Jam

#5 One on One

#6 Show Time!

#7 Slam Dunk!

#8 Ball Hog

#9 Hang Time

Coming soon:
#11 Above the Rim

FOUL!

by
Hank Herman

BANTAM BOOKS
NEW YORK · TORONTO · LONDON · SYDNEY · AUCKLAND

RL 2.6, 007-010

FOUL!

A Bantam Book / April 1997

Produced by Daniel Weiss Associates, Inc.
33 West 17th Street
New York, NY 10011.

Cover art by Jeff Mangiat.

All rights reserved.

ISBN: 0-553-48432-X
Published simultaneously in the United States and Canada

Bantam Books are published by Bantam Books, a division of Bantam
Doubleday Dell Publishing Group, Inc. Its trademark, consisting of the
words "Bantam Books" and the portrayal of a rooster, is Registered in U.S.
Patent and Trademark Office and in other countries. Marca Registrada.
Bantam Books, 1540 Broadway, New York, New York 10036.

PRINTED IN THE UNITED STATES OF AMERICA

OPM   0 9 8 7 6 5 4 3 2 1

To Kat, Sarah, and Patty

CHAPTER 1

"If we're four and one, and the Slashers are four and one, then we're tied for first place," David Danzig said to Brian Simmons, who was sitting in the backseat of Mrs. Danzig's car.

"*Duh*," Brian replied sarcastically, though with a grin on his face. "Dave, you're a genius."

"Excuse me, guys," Mrs. Danzig cut in. "David, could you please roll your window back up? It's freezing outside, and I have the heater on."

Dave waited a few seconds, as if he hadn't heard what his mother said.

Then slowly, deliberately, he opened the window even wider.

"David, I thought I asked you—"

"All right already!" Dave grumbled as he angrily rolled the window back up. He *hated* it when she called him David. "You keep the temperature at about a hundred degrees in this heap all the time. I'm gonna suffocate if I keep the window closed."

Mrs. Danzig looked across the front seat at her son. Dave could tell that she was thinking about giving him a reproachful answer. But then she obviously changed her mind, because she just shook her head and didn't say anything.

Dave knew it wasn't *her* fault she had to drive the beat-up red Plymouth. When his dad, an English professor, had died of a heart attack a few years ago, he hadn't exactly left them with a pile of money. And his mom's job at the Branford Public Library didn't earn her an All-Pro salary either. Still, he just couldn't seem to stop acting mean to her lately.

Dave pushed his long blond hair out of his face with his right hand and returned to his conversation with Brian.

"As we were saying before you-know-who interrupted us"—Dave glanced at his mother—"if we're tied for first with the Sampton Slashers, then who's next?"

"Well, let's see," Brian said thoughtfully, rubbing his hand over his short fade haircut. "I think Portsmouth and Harrison are both three and two—"

"That makes 'em tied for second," Dave broke in.

"No, dummy, tied for *third*," Brian corrected. "You're not so good at this higher math, are you?"

Brian Simmons could get away with saying anything he wanted to Dave. Brian and Dave were next-door neighbors and had been playing basketball together since kindergarten. The two of them—along with Will Hopwood—were the original members of the

Branford Bulls, a team of basketball-crazy fifth-graders from Benjamin Franklin Middle School.

"Okay, so those are the four teams in the race," Dave went on, ignoring his friend's remark. "One team we don't have to worry about catching us is that sorry group we're playing today. Has Winsted even won a game yet this season?"

"Yeah, they're one and four," Brian answered. "They beat Essex a few weeks ago in the battle of the losers."

Mrs. Danzig guided the old Plymouth into the parking lot of the Winsted Community Center, where the Winsted Wildcats played their home games. The Bulls always played on the road, since Branford was the only town in the Danville County Basketball League that didn't have its own community gym.

"What's this obsession with the standings?" Mrs. Danzig asked innocently. "The season's not even half over yet."

"Mom, why don't you ever know *anything?*" Dave asked with exasperation.

His rude outburst drew a sharp glance from Brian. Dave knew that Brian liked his mother a lot. *All* the Bulls did. Mrs. Danzig came to every game and always had encouraging things to say, even if the Bulls were playing lousy. She was short and pretty, with the same blond hair and blue eyes as Dave. The Bulls knew that "Mrs. D." would do anything for them.

"It's the Danville County March Madness contest," Brian said quickly, trying to cut off any other sharp words between Dave and his mother. "Whichever team is in first place by March first goes to the NCAA Final Four in Indianapolis and gets to sit in front-row seats. It would be unbelievably awesome! And we have a real good shot at it."

"That *is* unbelievable," Mrs. Danzig answered. "All the more reason you've got to beat the Wildcats today, right?" she continued.

"No problem," Brian replied. "The Wildcats don't even belong on the same floor with the Bulls. All we've got to do is hit a decent number of shots and play a little D."

"Speaking of D," Mrs. Danzig said in a tone that was half kidding, half serious, "I noticed that's the grade David got on his *Old Yeller* test. I'm sorry to bring this up in front of Brian, but you wouldn't listen to me this morning."

Dave gave her a threatening look, as if to ask, *What were you doing looking through my work?*

"Last night, when you said you thought your gloves were in your backpack, I went looking for them," his mother said, answering his unspoken question. "I saw the test and the comments Ms. Darling wrote on your paper: 'You can do a lot better than this if you put forth a little effort.'"

"What did you do, memorize what she wrote?" Dave growled. "Man, it wasn't even a test, it was a *quiz!* Besides, it's Saturday. Can't you stop bugging me about school for a *day,* or is that too much to ask?"

Mrs. Danzig had pulled into a parking spot about fifty yards from the entrance to the community center. She turned off the ignition and faced her son.

"You know," she started, "ever since your dad died—"

"I've become more and more of a wise guy," Dave cut in, sarcastically finishing her sentence for her. *How many times do we have to go through this?* he wondered.

"Well, it's true," his mother said. "And at the same time, your behavior on the basketball court has gotten worse. And your grades are going down, down, down—especially in English. David, what's gotten into you?"

Dave didn't answer her question. He knew his mother was right. His behavior *had* gotten worse after his dad died. Well, it wasn't *exactly* after his dad died. For a while Dave had tried to pretend his dad was still alive—that he hadn't died of a heart attack but was just off on a long trip somewhere. It was only when Dave's good friend Mr. Bowman, the friendly proprietor of Bowman's Market, *also* had a heart attack scare that Dave finally came to grips with the fact that his father was gone.

But it hadn't been until a month ago—when the Danville County Basketball League staged a father-son tournament—that he really began acting resentful. Mrs. Danzig hadn't wanted Dave to have to go alone, so she participated in place of Dave's father. And did Dave ever hear about having his *mom* play in the father-son game! Some of the more obnoxious kids in the league still reminded him about it when their teams played the Bulls.

Somehow Dave couldn't seem to forgive his mom for that. And even though he knew it made no sense, he found himself blaming his mother for the fact that he no longer had a father.

As the silence dragged on, Dave noticed Brian squirming in the backseat, looking as though he desperately wanted to open the car door and make a run for it.

"Mom, would you give me a break?" Dave finally hissed at his mother. He was furious at her for bringing up the topic again. Under his breath he added, "You know, we're not the only ones in this car." He cast a significant look in Brian's direction.

Mrs. Danzig raised her eyebrows, and there was a trace of a smile on her face. Dave could see she wasn't buying his concern for Brian's feelings.

"If you'd listened to me this morning, we wouldn't have to go through this now," Mrs. Danzig reminded him. "And anyway, Brian's your best friend. I'm sure he's heard all of this before."

Brian nodded, as if to say, *Many times!*

All three got out of the car and

walked toward the building's entrance. Dave was wearing a ski jacket, but he could feel the cold on his legs. He never wore sweats, even in the dead of winter. He wore the same long, droopy shorts all year round.

Before the two boys ran off to join their teammates, Mrs. Danzig put a hand on Dave's shoulder. "I hope the Bulls win, and I hope you have a good game," she said in a gentle voice. "But just remember: If your grades don't pick up, and if your behavior both on and off the court doesn't improve, we're going to have to make some changes."

Dave glowered at his mother. "Can I go now?"

A wounded look crossed Mrs. Danzig's face. "Yes, honey," she answered. "You can go."

Hey, Mom, great timing for a lecture like that, Dave silently told her as he stalked into the gym. *Just what I need to think about before a must-win game!*

CHAPTER 2

Dave noticed the wet snow the Bulls had tracked onto the shiny wood floor as he and Brian walked toward the visiting team's

bench. Some of his teammates wore old sneakers to the game, then changed into their good ones once inside, but Dave didn't bother. Too much trouble, he figured.

"Hey, guys, nice job of wiping your feet outside!"

Dave looked down to the other end of the gym, where the Wildcats were warming up. He had a pretty good idea of who had yelled the sarcastic comment. Sure enough, he saw Jason Fox grinning his wise-guy grin. The Wildcats' forward had a flat nose, eyes set close together, and straight black hair. Jason was no taller than Dave, but he was built like a truck. Dave always found him really obnoxious.

"I mean, we *are* trying to play basketball here," Fox continued.

Dave was about to reply, but Mark Fisher, the only Bull with a quicker tongue than Dave, beat him to it.

"You're always *trying* to play basketball," Mark said with a wicked smile. "It's just that you don't *do* it very well." Mark pulled off his prescription 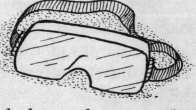 goggles and wiped them clean on the front of his jersey. Then he added,

"What have you guys got? One win over Essex? When we beat Essex, we don't even bother counting it as a win."

Mark looked around at his teammates for approval, and a few of the Bulls snickered. But Jim, one of the Bulls' two teenage coaches, silenced them with a glare. Jim was a star guard on Branford High's varsity team and was also Will Hopwood's older brother. Dave knew Jim hated it when the Bulls got dragged into these trash-talking sessions.

"Come on, guys," Jim said in a no-nonsense voice, clapping his hands. "Let's get down to business."

The Bulls ripped off their heavy winter jackets and their sweats and dumped them in a pile on the floor at the end of the visitors' bench. Then they went right into their three-man weave. They did this drill better than any other team in the league. The ball whizzed quickly and sharply from player to player, never touching the floor. Dave, Brian, Will, Derek

Roberts, and Jo Meyerson—the five starters—were especially smooth, but Mark, Chunky Schwartz, and MJ Jordan were no slouches either.

The Wildcats, down at the other basket, were doing a layup drill of their own, but Dave could see that Jason Fox was watching the Bulls. He knew Jason had to be impressed by the red-and-blue blur of the Bulls' uniforms and the screech of flying sneakers.

"Man, look at those Bulls work that pretty weave," Dave heard Fox say. Fox was talking to Ron Rice, the Wildcats' center, but what he said was obviously meant for the Bulls to hear. "Too bad that weave means squat in a game. Hey, Ron, didn't we *beat* the Bulls when we played 'em last summer? Or has my memory gotten all screwed up?"

No, his memory's fine—how could anyone *forget that game?* Dave thought. Jim Hopwood and Nate Bowman, the Bulls' other coach, had been away at a basketball camp and had left the team in the hands of Will and Brian. But Will and Brian had gotten into a fight, and . . . Dave didn't even want to think about it. It was too embarrassing.

The two teams finished warming up, then huddled with their coaches. The warning buzzer sounded, and both starting fives walked out onto the court. Dave found a place around the center circle and shook his long blond hair away from his face.

Seeing this, Jason nudged Ron. "Looks like they have *two* girls on their team," Fox said with a sneer. He was looking at Dave and Jo Meyerson, the Bulls' other guard. Jo was the only female starting player in the league.

Dave remembered his mom's warning about his behavior on the

court, but he couldn't restrain himself. "Come on, Foxy, you jerk, why don't you try to guard me man-to-man?" he challenged. "Then we'll see who's still talking trash at the end of the game."

But the Wildcats' bulky forward took his place alongside Brian for the center jump.

"No, thanks, cutie," Fox shot back. "I think I'll play someone who might actually be able to score. Not someone who has to hold his mother's hand at the father-son game."

Dave's face turned bright red. He clenched both fists and started in the direction of the sturdily built forward. But Brian stepped in front of him, blocking his path.

"Hey," his teammate warned, "save your energy for the game!"

Dave brought the ball upcourt with less than a minute remaining in the third quarter. The score was 28–28.

Why do we always play down to the

Wildcats' level? Dave wondered. *Losing today won't exactly help our chances for the March Madness contest. . . .*

Dave desperately wanted to work the ball in to Will in the pivot. But even though Will had two inches on Ron Rice, the Wildcats' center was playing in front of him and had been able to deny Will the ball all game. Now Ron had Will blanketed again.

Fortunately, Dave saw Brian break free in the left corner and quickly fired a pass to him. Brian, without hesitating, launched a fadeaway jumper, but it fell way short.

What's wrong with us? Dave worried. *That shot from Brian is usually money in the bank.* Dave thought about how Jim often told the Bulls that if they had one flaw, it was that they took the weak teams too lightly.

That criticism certainly seemed on target in this case!

Gene Walker, the Wildcats' other forward and their best all-around player, hauled in Brian's missed shot. The tall African American kid with rippling muscles tried to trigger a fast break. But the Bulls got back to their defensive end of the floor quickly, and the Wildcats were forced to set up their offense.

After several tosses around the perimeter, one of the Winsted guards was finally able to sneak a bounce pass to Rice in the paint. The Wildcats' center turned and attempted to shoot over Will, but Will caught him on the wrist as he tried for the block.

"Foul, number fourteen," the ref barked, extending a muscular arm in Will's direction. "Two shots."

Dave recognized the referee as Mr. Sparks, a short African American man with an athletic build. He had called a lot of the Bulls' games and was one of the best refs in the league.

Rice went to the line. Without a lot of fanfare, he made his first shot cleanly, giving the Wildcats a 29–28 lead. But he shot the second a little too hard, and the ball clanged off the back iron. Derek, the Bulls' tall, razor-thin forward, leaped high to grab the rebound.

Dave, sensing the opportunity for a fast break, went streaking toward the Bulls' basket. The always alert Derek hit him with a one-hand baseball-style outlet pass. Dave saw just one olive-and-red Wildcats jersey between him and the basket. Jason Fox, antici-pating the break, had hustled back on defense and stationed himself at the foul line.

Dave knew he could easily pass off to either Brian or Derek to beat the lone defender and score the go-ahead hoop. But he was still fuming over Fox's wise remarks at the start of the game.

This opportunity is too good to miss, he thought. Picking up steam as he approached the foul line, he rammed hard into Fox with his body. Dave used his left palm to straight-arm the huskier boy in the face—and still managed to get the layup off with his right hand.

It went in!

"No basket!" Mr. Sparks shouted, running toward Dave while holding his hand to the back of his head, indicating the violation. "That's a charge on number eleven! *And* a technical foul, for unsportsmanlike conduct!"

Dave hung his head. He realized instantly what a stupid move he'd made. *We could have had an easy fast-break layup and taken the lead,* he thought. *But after I manhandled Jason Fox like that, of course Mr. Sparks had to call me for a T. So my basket doesn't count, and the Wildcats go to the line. And in a tight game like this . . .*

His teammates' reactions didn't help matters. "Smart move," Will muttered sarcastically, shaking his head.

Dave usually bristled when Will acted like a know-it-all. But this time he could only shrug in agreement.

Mr. Sparks cleared the area around the foul line in order for the Wildcats to take the technical. The Winsted coach had chosen Gene Walker to shoot the T.

As Gene strode confidently to the foul line, Dave stood back near midcourt. He stole a look at his mother in the bleachers. She was staring

21

straight down, not even looking at the game. It was at times like this—when his mother wasn't yelling at him but was obviously really hurt by what he'd done—that Dave felt the most ashamed. *And* the most angry.

Walker made the technical.

A few seconds later the third quarter ended, with the Wildcats ahead 30–28.

Dave didn't need anyone to tell him that if he had only been able to keep his cool, it would have been the Bulls—not the Wildcats—holding the lead going into the final period.

"Show time!" the Bulls yelled,

breaking their huddle with their traditional war cry.

Dave knew the Bulls would really have to pick up the pace in the final period if they were going to put away the Wildcats. But within the first two minutes of play, Jo passed a ball off Will's foot, Brian missed an easy jumper from close range, and Dave himself blew an unchallenged layup. *It's just like Jim says,* Dave thought. *We don't take the Wildcats seriously.*

Derek was the only one of the Bulls who seemed to be able to hit anything. The smooth forward connected on a jumper, a fast-break layup, a put-back of a missed shot by Jo Meyerson, and a free throw. All by himself he scored seven of the nine points the Bulls put on the board in the fourth quarter.

Fortunately for the Bulls, the inept Wildcats were even more dismal than usual. After the team from Winsted missed its seventh straight shot of the quarter—most of them air balls—Brian looked at Dave, shook his head, and said under his breath, "Good thing we're not playing the Sampton Slashers today!"

The Bulls won—just barely. The final score was 37–34.

Dave looked for his mother as the Bulls jammed their drink bottles and warm-up shirts into their gym bags and gathered up their jackets. Their parents were making their way onto the floor, congratulating the Bulls on their narrow escape.

Dave kept looking around. "Anyone see my mom?" he called out to nobody in particular.

Nate Bowman, who had been busy stuffing basketballs into the Bulls' mesh ball bag, nodded in the direction of the upper bleachers.

Dave followed Nate's glance and spotted his mother. She hadn't moved from where she'd been sitting the whole game. She was saying something to Mrs. Simmons. Her expression was grim.

Man, Dave thought, *does she look miserable! Why do I keep torturing her like this?*

Dave and his teammates trailed Nate Bowman out to the parking lot. The plan, as usual, was to pile into the Bowman's Market van—known as the Bullsmobile—and head over to

Bowman's for their victory sodas.

Dave noticed that Nate's footprints in the snow looked almost twice the

size of his own. *Guess when you wear size-seventeen sneakers, you make pretty big tracks*, he thought.

Nate, along with Jim Hopwood, was co-captain of Branford High's basketball team. The tall senior, who wore a gold stud earring, was probably the best high-school basketball player in the county. All the Bulls idolized him, and Dave wanted nothing more than to wear a blue-and-white varsity jacket just like the one Nate was wearing. Only his would have his own number, eleven, on the sleeve, instead of Nate's twenty-two.

Nate put his huge hand on the top of the red-and-black Chicago Bulls knit cap Dave wore on his head. "Droopy," he said, calling Dave by his nickname, "you guys came *this close* to blowing that game." He held the thumb and index finger of his right hand about a half inch apart. "Imagine if we had to go back to the store and tell my dad you lost to a team as sorry as the Winsted

27

Wildcats—again!" The whole time he was talking, Nate wore his trademark ear-to-ear smile.

Dave knew just what he was talking about. Nate Bowman, Sr., was probably the most loyal Branford Bulls fan in town. Another loss to the lowly Wildcats would have horrified him.

"I wasn't worried for a minute," Jo Meyerson said matter-of-factly. She wore a bulky neon green-and-blue ski parka, dark blue nylon warm-up pants to cover her skinny legs, and—as always—a green baseball cap, worn backward. "I knew we had Superman here to bail us out." Jo clapped Derek on the back. "Seven out of our nine points in the last quarter himself. Not a bad performance."

Derek allowed his lips to turn up into something that almost looked like a smile. Dave knew that was about as close as the quiet star of the Bulls would ever come to congratulating himself.

"Hey, we just like to make things

exciting," Dave added, continuing the banter.

"A little more excitement like that and you guys will play yourselves right out of first place." Jim Hopwood, as usual, was trying to keep the Bulls in touch with reality. Dave noticed that Jim didn't even have a smile on his face. Dave was always amazed at the difference in outlook between the two coaches. Nate could be grinning and goofing around with the Bulls down by ten, while Jim would barely allow himself to smile if they were up by twenty!

Just before they reached the Bullsmobile, Dave heard the sound of sneakers crunching on packed snow. He turned to see MJ, the Bulls' least talented but most basketball-wise sub, running toward them.

"Y-You're not going to believe this," MJ stammered, out of breath.

"Okay, I don't believe it," Mark Fisher cracked.

"Seriously," MJ continued, "I was

just talking to Mr. Peroni, the Wildcats' coach. His brother coaches the Harrison Hornets. He told me the Hornets beat the Slashers today!"

"So?" Chunky Schwartz asked. Chunky, the Bulls' backup center, was as wide as he was tall—and was sometimes a little slow on the uptake when it came to basketball matters.

"So it means the Branford Bulls are in sole possession of first place!" Will Hopwood exclaimed. Will was right up there with MJ in basketball smarts—and way ahead of him in talent. As a matter of fact, the Bulls' five-foot-four center was one of the top two players on the team, second only to Derek Roberts.

"How do you figure?" Dave asked, leaning on the hood of the Bullsmobile. For some reason, he was having an impossible time keeping the league's standings straight.

"Okay, let me walk you through this one more time," Brian said with exaggerated slowness, like a teacher talking to a

30

particularly dense student. "We won today, so we're five and one. Sampton's loss drops them to four and two—same as Harrison, with their win. We haven't heard about the Portsmouth Panthers yet, but they were playing Rochester, so let's assume they won. That would make them four and two also. That's three teams tied for second, and all alone in first . . ." Brian patted himself on the back. "Us!"

"It's lonely at the top," Mark kidded as he slid the door of the van open.

"So if we beat Portsmouth next week," Dave continued, thinking out loud, "then we clinch the league lead as of March first, and we snag the trip to the Final Four!"

Brian looked heavenward, as if what Dave had just said was incredibly obvious. "Boy's a genius," Brian said simply.

The players continued to whoop it up and kid each other as they piled into the Bullsmobile. Just as Dave was about to climb in, he felt a hand on his shoulder.

It was his mother.

"I hate to do this to you, David," Mrs. Danzig said, "but you have to come home with me and study. We've got to do something about your grades."

Judging from the somber expression on her face, Dave knew this was about more than just bad grades.

"Study on a Saturday?" Dave asked. "Don't hold your breath," he added in a wise-guy tone, for the benefit of his teammates.

Mrs. Danzig bit her lip. "I really don't like to embarrass you in front of your friends, David, but I told you to watch your behavior before the game—and look what happened," she said, her tone serious. "I'm going to tell you something, and the whole team might as well hear it. One more technical foul, or one more grade below a C, and you're grounded for a month! Now let's go."

She turned and began walking through the crusty snow toward her car.

Dave took one last look at his teammates in the Bullsmobile and gave them a shrug, as if to say, *No big deal*. Then he jammed his hands into the pockets of his parka and followed his mother.

But though he'd tried to act cool in the presence of his friends, he felt humiliated and furious. *I'd rather* walk *back to Branford*, he thought, *than ride in that old red Plymouth with* her!

"All right, calm down," Ms. Darling said.

In a matter of seconds, all the kids in the class settled into their seats and the room became quiet. Dave couldn't believe how she managed to do that. Other teachers would yell and scream, and nobody listened. Ms. Darling didn't even raise her voice, and everyone did what she wanted them to do.

It didn't hurt, Dave supposed, that she was pretty. Or that she wore cool clothes. And for the jocks in the class—including Dave, Brian, and

Derek—it didn't hurt that she was a basketball freak. Behind her desk hung a huge poster of Dennis Rodman, his green hair glowing.

If he had to be in school on Monday morning, Dave could think of worse places to be than in Ms. Darling's English class.

Now that she had the attention of the students, Ms. Darling reviewed what the homework assignment had been for that day: Write three paragraphs about something that had made a big impression on you over the weekend.

"Can I have a volunteer to read what he or she has written?" Ms. Darling asked.

Jordan, a tall girl who wore her brown hair in a long ponytail, shot her hand in the air.

Dave fell off his seat, pretending to be in shock.

"Okay, Dave, what's the matter?" Ms. Darling asked, a hand on her hip.

"It's just that I'm so amazed that

Jordan asked to be the first to read," Dave said, his voice heavy with sarcasm. A bunch of the kids in the back row giggled. Jordan was a notorious brownnoser.

Ms. Darling gave Dave a frozen smile and didn't say anything, but it couldn't have been more clear that she didn't find his antics funny. Dave knew that though Ms. Darling had a great sense of humor, she didn't like it when one student ridiculed another.

Jordan ignored Dave's remark and walked up to the front of the room. Dave noticed that she was almost as tall as Ms. Darling—which wasn't saying much, since Ms. Darling was pretty short. Jordan cleared her throat, tossed her head back dramatically, and began reading her assignment.

As near as Dave could follow, Jordan's essay had to do with driving past a church on Saturday afternoon and witnessing a big wedding celebration. Jordan went on and on about the beautiful bride, the handsome groom, and the bridesmaids' purple dresses.

Dave looked across the room and caught sight of Brian faking a yawn. Both of them began laughing hysterically. Dave knew that once he started laughing that way, there was no way to stop. He tried his best to hide his face behind his hands, but it was no use. Ms. Darling didn't miss a trick.

"You know that's why I put the two of you on opposite sides of the room," Ms. Darling said to Dave and Brian. Though she used a scolding tone, Dave could see the hint of a smile on her face. *She probably thinks Jordan's essay is pretty drippy too,* Dave figured.

"Since you seem to need something to keep you awake this morning, Brian," Ms. Darling continued, "why don't you be next to read your essay to the class?"

Brian gave a here-goes-nothing shrug, stood up alongside his seat, and started reading. His piece was about a fight he'd seen between Todd and Allie, his little brother and sister, who were twins. He gave a lot of details about the fierce look on Todd's face and the "wild right hook" thrown by Allie.

As Brian read, the wise-guy tone he'd started with left his voice, and his dark eyes sparkled.

Dave could see that Ms. Darling was impressed. Brian was a pretty good English student; he usually got B-pluses or A-minuses.

"That was great, Brian!" Ms. Darling said enthusiastically when he finished reading. "Why do you think that fight made such a strong impression on you?"

"Well," Brian answered slowly, "I guess I never knew a girl could kick a boy's butt the way Allie kicked Todd's!"

The whole class laughed, and so did Ms. Darling. "Well, it's about time you learned that lesson!" she said, smiling broadly.

The next few students took their

turns. Though Dave was pretty sure there was nothing that great about their essays, he noticed that Ms. Darling gave special praise and specific suggestions to each reader. *She really* is *a good teacher,* he thought.

A little more than halfway through the class, Ms. Darling called on Derek to read his essay.

A look of panic crossed Derek's face. Dave knew why. It wasn't that Derek was unprepared or that he was a poor English student—in fact, he got straight A's. It was just that Derek was so private. *We can hardly get this guy to open his mouth on the basketball court,* Dave thought. *He sure isn't going to want to read in front of a packed classroom!*

Derek got up reluctantly, as if he were facing a firing squad. Though he was fairly tall, it was hard to tell, because he didn't really stand up straight. He sort of leaned against his chair for support.

When he began reading, his voice

was barely more than a whisper.

"Come on, Derek, speak up!" Ms. Darling encouraged. "Pretend you just took a hard foul from the Sampton Slashers."

Derek gave a slight smile and spoke a tiny bit louder. Dave had to tilt his head in order to hear at all. Derek was reading about a squirrel and a bird feeder. Dave had absolutely no idea why Derek had chosen to write about that.

When Derek finished, he sat back down quickly and looked at his feet.

Ms. Darling paused a moment. Then she said, "Derek, that was beautiful. *Absolutely beautiful.*" Then, looking at the class, she added, "I wonder if you all appreciate what Derek was reading about—how he first tried to chase the squirrel away from the feeder but then realized that the squirrel had a right to eat too."

She took a deep breath. "Derek, if you don't mind, I'm going to hold on to your paper so that I can read it to the next class."

Derek shrugged, continuing to stare down at his shoes. Dave could see how embarrassed he was.

"Way to go, Shakespeare," he kidded Derek under his breath.

"What was that?" Ms. Darling asked Dave sharply. When Dave didn't answer, she said, "We haven't heard from *you* yet, Dave. I'm sure you'd like to be the one to go after Derek."

"Well, I didn't see any squirrels or bird feeders this weekend," Dave muttered as he slowly unfolded himself from his seat. "But here goes." He began to read. "'On Saturday we played the Winsted Wildcats. I stank. Our whole team stank. Luckily, the Wildcats stank worse. Final Four, here we come!'" He lowered the paper and looked up at Ms. Darling.

"That's *it?*" she asked.

Dave nodded. Almost everybody in the class laughed, and Dave bowed to them.

But Ms. Darling wasn't amused. "I thought I made it pretty clear I wanted three paragraphs," she said.

"Here, look," Dave replied, walking forward and bringing her his paper. "I made each sentence a separate paragraph. That's *five* paragraphs."

Ms. Darling rolled her eyes. "And why did this game make such an impression on you? The Bulls play *every* Saturday."

"Well, this time we *really* stank," Dave answered. "You should have seen us."

He expected Ms. Darling to laugh. She usually laughed at his jokes.

But not this time.

"See me after class, Dave," she said, and turned to the next reader.

"Dave, you know I think you're a pretty cool kid," Ms. Darling said to him when they were alone in the classroom.

He felt his face flush.

"But this behavior of yours has gone too far," she continued. "Brian goofs around too—but at least he does good work."

"You're beginning to sound like my mother," Dave commented.

"Well, I'm not your mother, I'm your teacher. And I'm telling you, you're much smarter than you let on. I've seen things you've written in the past that were excellent. But what you turned in last week on the *Old Yeller* exam? Come on, Dave. You were lucky I gave you a D."

"Thanks," Dave said sarcastically.

"The way you act in this class, sometimes it's hard to believe your father was an English professor. . . ."

Dave's face turned bright red. He hated it when people brought up his father.

"You know, with just a little effort," Ms. Darling continued, "you could be doing as well in English as Derek."

Dave just snickered.

Ms. Darling, however, didn't let up. "Why don't you come in and work on an extra-credit paper?" she pursued. Seeing the look of distaste on his face, she added, "We could shoot some hoops while you work."

Dave knew Ms. Darling's suggestion made some sense. He remembered what his mother had said to him outside the Bullsmobile after the Winsted game: *One more technical foul, or one more grade below a C, and you're grounded for a month.* And he was clearly headed for a grade below a C.

Still, he wasn't going to fall for his teacher's offer. His mouth turned down in a scornful sneer. "Extra-credit papers," he proclaimed, "are for dorks and kiss-ups."

"Dave, just because you do a paper, it doesn't mean—"

"I don't mean to disrespect you, Ms. Darling," Dave interrupted, "but I can tell you right now that you'll make it to the NBA before you ever see a Branford Bull turn in an extra-credit paper."

Dave slung his backpack over his right shoulder and hurried out the door, late for his next class.

"No, no, Dave!" Jim called in exasperation, hitting himself on the head with both hands. "I wanted you to call the play where *Brian's* the shooter. That's number *three!*"

Dave didn't know why he always froze when it came to remembering the plays. Dribbling and passing—that came naturally. Shooting and playing tough D he could handle too. But running the set plays . . . sometimes he found himself wishing he weren't the point guard.

"Okay, I've got it straight now, Coach," he said. "Sorry."

45

"Good thing it's only a practice," Dave heard Jim mutter under his breath. "Okay, run it again," Jim called out, "the *right* way this time." He threw the ball hard to Dave.

Dave's hands stung as he caught it. Though the afternoon was sunny and relatively warm for February, it still wasn't exactly what Dave would consider ideal weather for hoops. Since the Bulls didn't have access to an indoor gym for practice, they had to hold their workouts on the blacktop court in Jefferson Park. They liked this setup fine in the spring, summer, and fall— but in the middle of winter, a nice cozy gym wouldn't have been bad at all.

Though a few of the Bulls—namely Mark and Chunky—had been complaining about the cold all week, Dave was thankful the snow had finally melted so the team could practice. He knew the Portsmouth Panthers, their opponents the next day, were always tough. And he knew the Bulls needed a win to clinch the trip to Indianapolis.

Dave readied himself to run the play Jim had called. He held up the middle three fingers of his left hand as he dribbled with his right above the top of the key. He also called out, "Three!" nice and loud, to make doubly sure everyone knew what was supposed to happen.

Like clockwork, Will, who'd been playing the pivot, took a few quick steps to join Derek to the left of the paint, forming a double screen. Brian, who'd been playing right forward, ran across the lane to move behind the screen.

Just as Brian emerged from behind Will and Derek, Dave fired him the ball—but a large hand knocked it out of bounds and into the brown grass.

Dave groaned loudly. He couldn't figure out how the play had gotten botched up.

"Come on, Fadeaway," Nate said, using Brian's nickname. "You've got to run a lot closer to those guys when you use them as a screen. I was able to stay with you the whole time." It was Nate, Brian's defender, who had stepped in to deflect the pass.

"Yeah, but Coach," Brian pointed out, "you knew the play—*and* you're a good defender. When we play Portsmouth tomorrow, they *won't* know the play. And besides, that dumb, slow-moving Porky Kolodny will be playing me. He couldn't find his way around a pick with a road map!"

All the Bulls—including Nate— laughed at Brian's remark. But Dave could see that Jim was not amused.

"You know, Brian," Jim started, "you can goof on Porky Kolodny and the Panthers all you want, but tomorrow you've got to show me what you can do with the ball, not with your mouth." Then he addressed the team as a whole. "You guys have been talking an awful lot of trash lately. I noticed it before the Winsted game last Saturday, and what did we do? We barely escaped with a three-point win—against one of the worst teams in the league. And you know why? Because you goofed around in practice and didn't take them seriously. Just like you're doing now."

The Bulls listened in silence, some of them looking Jim in the eye, some of them staring off into the bare trees that surrounded the blacktop. Dave knew that when Jim got into one of these moods, it was best not to answer back.

"Okay, let's wrap it up," Jim said finally, his tone suddenly more upbeat. "Why don't you go play your game of Horse? I know you won't consider it a real practice unless you end it that way."

As the Bulls got in line for their ritual wrap-up, Jim grabbed Dave by the sleeve of his sweatshirt and pulled him to the edge of the blacktop. "Droopy," he said, "we've got to talk to you for a sec."

Nate was going to be in on this conversation also, Dave could see. *What now?* he thought. *I'm already in trouble with my mother and Ms. Darling. Now the coaches are ganging up on me too?*

Seeing the concerned look on Dave's face, Nate said, "Don't worry, Droopy, it's no big deal."

"Not a big deal, but it *is* important," Jim added. "Here's the thing, Dave. You've always had a temper, and that's cool—especially when it makes you play harder. But lately you've been blowing up during every game, and we can't afford that. You're the point guard. You're the guy who's supposed to be controlling the game for us."

Dave smiled sheepishly. "You mean that stupid shoving match I got into with Jason Fox last game?" he asked. Then he shrugged. "I guess I just snapped."

"Well, you can't *let* yourself just snap," Jim ordered.

"Remember—next technical foul and you're grounded for a month," added Will, who'd been hanging around the blacktop just close enough to listen in on the conversation.

Dave hated the way Will felt he had to get involved in everything. *Just because his brother's a coach . . .*

"Will, butt out!" he said angrily.

Jim didn't say anything, but he gave his brother a threatening look, and Will returned to the game of Horse.

"You know, Dave, Will's right," Jim said. "We all heard your mother say it. And we don't want to see you grounded—for the *team's* sake as well as your own."

Dave stood silently on the blacktop, taking in what Jim was saying.

Then, without warning, Nate bent over, palmed a basketball with his huge right hand, took three giant strides, and slam-dunked the ball in the basket where the rest of the team was playing Horse.

All the Bulls gawked, as they always did when Nate showed off like that.

"Top that, dudes!" Nate called out with a wide smile. Dave knew that was his way of saying, *Lecture's over*.

Dave joined the game of Horse. On his first try, he drove toward the hoop from the right, jumped, and, while spinning completely around, threw the ball up over his head. Somehow it hit the backboard and fell in.

But in the end, Derek won—as usual.

As the Bulls grabbed their parkas from the pile at the edge of the blacktop, Dave heard his name being called again. It was Nate.

The tall teenager wrapped his long arm around Dave's shoulder and said,

"One more word to the wise. You know that tall referee with the mustache—Mr. Spinelli? He's going to be calling our game tomorrow. Now, he's one of the best refs in the league, but do you remember anything special about him?"

"How could I forget?" Dave replied with a laugh. "Every time I touch the ball he calls me for traveling!"

"Well, not *every* time," Nate corrected. "He just doesn't let you get away with that little half step you like to take when you start your dribble."

Dave waited. So far he hadn't heard anything he didn't already know.

"Now the best thing you could do," Nate went on, "is to try to eliminate that little step. But if you can't and he calls you for it, you've got to try to be cool."

"Well, even though he's wrong every time he calls it on me," Dave said stubbornly, "I'll be cool. Cool as ice."

"All right, Ice," Nate said. "Gimme five!"

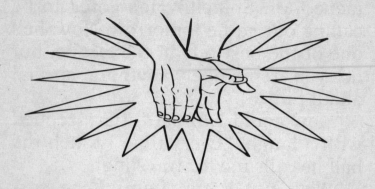

Dave slapped him a low five, the Bulls' trademark. Then he ran to join the rest of the Bulls as they headed up the paved path to the gates of Jefferson Park.

"Show time!" the Bulls yelled before they headed out to begin the game.

Dave sauntered onto the floor, tossing his blond hair out of his eyes. He tugged his dark blue shorts so the bottoms hung down below his knees. He loved this part of the game—strutting out on the court with the starting five of the Branford Bulls, with the whole crowd watching. The lights in the Portsmouth gym seemed particularly bright to Dave. He felt almost as if he were onstage, performing under a spotlight.

Dave heard a roar from the other end of the gym. It was the Panthers yelling, "Win!" as they took the court. He hated to admit it, but they looked pretty cool too in their black-and-gray uniforms.

The Panthers lined up the way the Bulls had anticipated. Sure enough, Porky Kolodny, a heavyset kid with a red crew cut and a dumb expression on his face, lumbered over alongside Brian. The kid everyone called Bucky, the Panthers' tall center and top scorer, matched up with Will. And—also no surprise—Air Ball Archibald, the stocky but quick point guard, covered Dave.

Dave knew he'd have a fairly easy

time on D, since Air Ball—as his nickname suggested—was a terrible shooter. But he was a tough, scrappy defender. *Between Air Ball's defense and Mr. Spinelli's reffing,* Dave thought, *I could be in for a long afternoon.*

The gym was a little more crowded than usual. Since this was a game between two contenders, Dave could see that a few kids from other teams in the league had actually shown up. Of course, most of the parents of the players were there too. Dave spotted his mom sitting, as usual, between Mr. and Mrs. Simmons and Mr. and Mrs. Hopwood.

Mr. Spinelli, towering above the two centers, tossed up the ball to begin the game. Will, with a slight height advantage over Bucky, outleaped him and tapped the ball to Dave.

Dave noticed that the Panthers were slow getting back to their defensive positions and saw an instant opportunity to slash to the hoop. But as soon as he began his drive he heard the screech of Mr. Spinelli's whistle. The tall ref with the mustache rotated his arms one over the other, slowly, indicating the traveling call.

Dave hated how dramatically the ref went through the motion. *He looks like an old-fashioned lawn mower,* Dave thought irritably. *Why doesn't he just say, "Traveling" and get it over with?*

Though Dave's first instinct was to run up to the referee's face and insist he wasn't traveling, he remembered what Jim and Nate had told him. Though he needed to physically put his hand over his mouth, he managed to fight the urge to protest, and he just handed the ball over to Mr. Spinelli.

As he jogged back to the Bulls' defensive end of the court, he caught Nate's eye. Nate nodded at him approvingly.

Bucky got things going quickly for the Panthers by hitting a short jumper on their first possession, but Derek came right back with a finger roll for the Bulls to even the score.

That was pretty much the pattern of the first quarter: two very good teams punching and counterpunching.

Midway through the second quarter, Brian got into one of his sizzling streaks, banging in three straight jumpers from the left corner. That gave the Bulls the lead, 25–21.

Porky, who'd been burned by Brian's three missiles, tried to bring the Panthers back rapidly by launching a twenty-footer from the top of the key, but his shot barely grazed the front of the rim. Derek was right there for the rebound and handed it off to Dave.

REBOUND!

Dave advanced the ball deliberately. A basket now would give the Bulls a six-point lead, their biggest of the game. Glancing over at the bench, Dave saw Jim's arm in the air, with all five fingers raised. Dave was pleased he remembered the play without any trouble. Five was the signal for a clear-out: All the Bulls would shift to the left side of the court, taking their defenders with them, leaving Dave alone on the right side to work one-on-one against Air Ball.

Dave raised his left arm, five fingers held high, as he dribbled with his right hand. As planned, Will, Derek, Brian, and Jo all slid over to the left—and the Panthers' defenders followed.

Air Ball Archibald, seeing all his teammates move to one side of the court, got confused and shifted over with them. Dave couldn't believe his eyes. He'd been left all alone, with a clear path to the basket!

Dave bounded immediately to the hoop, hoping to score before Air Ball came to his senses. But he'd barely launched himself toward the basket when he was stopped in his tracks by the loud shriek of the referee's whistle. He turned around, and there was

Mr. Spinelli going through that slow-motion traveling pantomime again.

"I did *not* travel!" Dave yelled at Mr. Spinelli before he could even think of controlling himself. "I dribbled before I took that first step. You'd have to be blind not to see that!" Dave's face was almost in Mr. Spinelli's—or at least as close as he could get, considering their height difference.

The referee tried to walk away from Dave to let him cool down, but Dave

ran around in front of him to plead his case some more.

Finally Mr. Spinelli said firmly, "Eleven, watch it! That's a travel. End of conversation."

As the referee handed the ball to Air Ball Archibald for the Panthers to take possession, Dave saw Jim motioning to him wildly. Dave walked over in the direction of the Bulls' bench.

"Put a lid on it!" Jim hissed at him through clenched teeth. "You're lucky Spinelli didn't call a technical on you for that performance. *I* would have!"

Dave ran back out on the floor, the tips of his ears burning with embarrassment.

Air Ball brought the ball upcourt for the Panthers. As he approached Dave he dribbled the ball with exaggerated care.

"See?" the stocky guard snickered. "It's easy. *First* you dribble. *Then* you move your feet."

Dave felt the blood rush to his face.

This dude is asking for it, he thought.

Air Ball didn't let up. "Keep watching me, Danzig," he purred. "Remember, first dribble. Then step."

Dave lashed out for the ball that Air Ball dribbled temptingly in front of him, but he caught the Panther on the arm.

"Reach-in, number eleven," he heard Mr. Spinelli call. "Black ball on the side."

Dave felt his temperature rise. Mr. Spinelli was watching him like a hawk. Jim had already lost patience with him. And now Air Ball was starting to goad him every time he got his hands on the ball.

Be cool, Nate had told him.

Yeah, right, Dave thought. *Easy for him to say.*

Early in the fourth quarter, Mr. Spinelli called Dave for his third travel of the game. Dave, who had received a pretty heated talking-to from Jim at halftime, just handed the ref the ball and walked away, the way he'd been told to do.

But as he crouched down to play defense he heard Air Ball's sneering voice. "Dribbling lessons tomorrow afternoon at three," the Panther taunted. "Half price for you, Danzig. You need 'em bad."

Dave, who was widely considered one of the top ball handlers in the league, was infuriated by Air Ball's remark. It took a supreme effort for him to curb his urge to slug Air Ball right there on the spot. In the back of his mind he could hear his mother's voice warning him: *One more technical foul and you're grounded for a month.*

Air Ball dribbled lazily above the top of the key, as if he were in no hurry at all. Dave relaxed on defense for just half a second, rocking back on his heels instead of staying up on his toes. At that instant Air Ball shifted into high gear, sailing right past Dave for an easy layup.

Without even looking, Dave could feel the eyes of all his teammates on him. He couldn't *believe* he'd let Air Ball burn him so badly!

Dave watched as Air Ball made a big show of bumping chests with Porky Kolodny and Bucky. Then, before dropping back on defense, Air Ball shoved his face within six inches of Dave's and whispered one word in his ear: "Toast."

Dave was no longer hearing his mother's warning about one more technical foul—or Jim's halftime lecture about staying cool. All he could hear echoing in his head was the word *toast,* whispered to him by the kid who'd just humiliated him in front of the whole gym.

"I've had enough garbage from you, you little loser!" Dave exploded as he shoved Air Ball hard in the chest with two hands, sending him reeling backward toward the bleachers.

Air Ball crumpled to the hard gym floor in a heap. For a moment he didn't move. The entire building went silent.

Then, slowly, the Panther guard picked himself up off the floor, testing his hands, his arms, his neck, making sure nothing was injured.

Dave felt his legs shaking, both from fear that he had seriously hurt the opposing player and from anger. *He had it coming to him,* Dave told himself.

Mr. Spinelli didn't even bother talking to Dave. After making sure that Air Ball was all right, the ref went straight over to Jim and Nate. "We can't have any of this," he said gravely. "That kind of nonsense could cause a serious injury. We've got a technical foul on number eleven—and he's out of the game!"

A technical? And ejection? Dave thought immediately of his mother's threat.

He looked pleadingly at Nate, his eyes asking, *Isn't there anything you can do?*

But Nate just shook his head sadly. Dave realized he'd finally gone too far.

As Mark went to the scorer's table to check in, Dave took a seat on the end of the Bulls' bench. Then, steeling himself, he looked up at the bleachers where his mother was sitting. For a moment he couldn't find her. He spotted Will's mother, and Brian's mother . . .

Finally he saw her. She was sitting with her face in her hands. He was pretty sure she was crying.

Dave's fury evaporated. It was replaced by a queasy sensation in the pit of his stomach. *I can't believe I've made my mother cry!* he thought. Deep down he knew that losing his father was every bit as hard on his mom as it was on him—and still he kept making her suffer by throwing these ridiculous temper tantrums!

He looked at his mother again and saw that she was trying to compose herself. *I really don't* mean *to hurt her,* he said to himself. *It's just that sometimes I get so* angry. . . .

How do Chunky and MJ manage to keep their sanity on the bench? Dave wondered, shifting uncomfortably. He couldn't bear it. *Here it is, crunch time—and I'm not out on the floor!*

Dave checked the electronic scoreboard on the wall way up above the Panthers' basket. It showed six minutes and twenty-two seconds left in the game, with the Bulls ahead, 42–39.

"A measly three-point lead, with almost a whole quarter to play,"

PANTHERS BULLS

39 42

Dave agonized. He was talking as much to himself as to MJ, who sat alongside him. "What if Mark screws up? If we lose, we'll be down to five and two—and tied with Portsmouth. They could still beat us out for the trip to the Big Dance—and it'll be all my fault!"

MJ watched Dave squirm. "Not used to this, are you?"

Dave shook his head.

MJ, who often acted the part of assistant coach as much as player, gave Dave a friendly shove. "We'll be all right," he said.

"Yeah? Swear?" Dave asked as he drummed his sneakers nervously on the shiny wood floor.

Nate, who'd been shouting encouragement to the five Bulls on the court, jumped into the conversation. "You have a short memory, Droopy my man," he said to Dave. "Have you already forgotten that last summer, before Jo made the team, Mark was a starter? And a pretty decent one!"

Dave hadn't thought of it that way, but Nate was right: Since Jo had arrived on the scene, Dave had gotten to thinking of Mark as one of the scrubs.

"You may be the man," Nate continued, putting a hand on Dave's shoulder, "but with Jo at the point and Mark at shooting guard, we're still cool. Trust me."

At *exactly* the moment Nate said, "Trust me," Mark hoisted up one of his trademark bombs. It was an ugly shot that he heaved up from his hipbone, like a shot put. But amazingly—as so often happened—it was right on target.

Mr. Spinelli threw his arms straight up in the air, indicating the three-pointer.

Dave, MJ, and Chunky all leaped off the Bulls' bench at the same time. Nate and Jim slapped a low five.

70

"All right! Forty-five to thirty-nine!" MJ shouted.

"Keep shootin', Mark!" Nate cheered in a booming voice. "You just keep puttin' 'em up!"

Dave found the cheerleading spirit of the bench crew contagious. His spirits began to rise. *Maybe my getting tossed won't make us blow this game after all,* he reasoned.

But his growing optimism was checked when Bucky hit an all-but-impossible shot. With Will all over him, Bucky ducked under Will's long arms and flung the ball up underhand. It seemed to *crawl* over the rim and into the basket.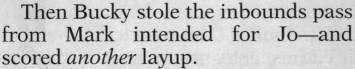

Then Bucky stole the inbounds pass from Mark intended for Jo—and scored *another* layup.

In the blink of an eye, the Bulls' lead was down to two: 45–43.

Jo stalled the Panthers' charge temporarily with a driving layup, but Graham Duckworth, the Panthers' handsome shooting guard who wore his black hair slicked back Pat Riley style, canned a twelve-footer. *Again* the Bulls' lead had been cut to two.

Dave's momentary elation vanished. Sitting on the bench was driving him crazy. The game got tighter and tighter—*and there was nothing he could do about it!* And every time the Panthers got close, Jim gave him a dirty look. Or at least so it seemed to Dave.

Dave glanced up at the scoreboard clock, as he did every few seconds. A minute and fifty-two seconds to go.

"Got a date?" Nate kidded him.

How can Nate be so cool when we're about to blow our chance to go to Indianapolis? Dave wondered.

With slightly more than a minute and a half to go in the game, Mark got ready to unload another bomb from downtown. Dave couldn't believe it. *Why not get the ball to Will or Derek now that we're getting down to the wire?*

Dave held his breath as his replacement's shot went up—*and in!* It was Mark's second three-pointer of the quarter!

THREE FROM DOWNTOWN!

"That should do it!" Dave crowed, leaping off the bench.

But less than ten seconds later, Porky Kolodny bulled his way through the Branford defense, made a layup—and was fouled by Brian.

FOUL!

"No way he makes this free throw," Chunky said hopefully.

Chunky, Dave, and MJ watched Porky's shot arc toward the basket.

"Way," MJ said mournfully as the ball fell cleanly through the hoop.

Once more the Bulls' lead was down to two.

"This is like Chinese water torture," MJ observed.

Out of the corner of his eye, Dave saw Jim giving him another dirty look. He could tell the coach's nerves were on edge. Jim didn't handle pressure nearly as well as Nate did.

"Where do you think you're more valuable to us?" Jim couldn't resist asking Dave. "Out on the court, or with your butt on the bench, where it is now?"

Dave knew better than to answer. Nate pushed Jim away from Dave, saying, "Easy, dude. Everything'll be cool."

But Dave knew that Jim was right. *I really screwed things up,* Dave thought. *Big-time!*

He checked the clock for about the twentieth time since he'd been kicked out of the game. Less than a minute left.

Mark made the inbounds pass to Jo under the Panthers' basket, being extra careful not to let it get picked off. Jo dribbled deliberately across mid-court. She was an excellent, sometimes fancy ball handler, but she wasn't trying anything tricky at this point in the game.

"Four, Jo," Dave heard Jim whisper hoarsely as the slim girl passed the Bulls' bench. "Call four."

Dave knew this was a play designed to get Derek open for a shot—a logical call at a critical time like this. And it worked. Derek, the Bulls' best player, was wide open twelve feet from the basket on the right side. Derek calmly squared up, and . . .

His shot was too hard and caromed off the back iron. *He always makes that shot!* Dave thought, shocked.

Bucky snared the rebound and handed off to Air Ball, who dribbled slowly upcourt. Dave was sure Portsmouth would try to set up their offense and work the ball in to Bucky for the game-tying basket.

But as the Panthers' point guard approached the top of the key, Dave couldn't believe what he was seeing. Air Ball himself—the worst shooter on the team—was putting up a three-pointer! Dave watched as the heave sailed high through the air.

Dave stared open-mouthed. MJ, Chunky, and Nate were stunned too. Only Jim had his wits about him, and he immediately asked Jo to call for a time-out.

Dave automatically checked the scoreboard. Twenty-eight seconds left. And for the first time since early in the first quarter, Portsmouth was ahead, 51–50.

"All right, lots of time, lots of time," Jim said in the huddle as he tried to keep the Bulls from panicking. He diagrammed a play for Will and carefully reviewed each player's role. The Bulls chanted their usual "Show time!" and headed back onto the floor.

Dave felt sick to his stomach. *That "Show time!" sounded pretty lame,* he thought. He also knew that in the last thirty seconds of a tight game, plays don't always work out the way they're designed on paper.

Jo was able to inbound the ball cleanly to Mark, but no matter what

Will tried to do in the paint, Bucky was all over him. He couldn't break free to receive the pass.

With the clock ticking—*twelve, eleven, ten*—Mark became desperate and finally went spinning to the hoop in a lunging drive. He was way off balance when he threw up a layup attempt, but fortunately he drew contact from Graham Duckworth.

"Number nineteen, black, with the foul," Mr. Spinelli called out. "Two shots."

Dave felt his heart pounding. *If only I could be out there instead of Mark!* he thought. With an amazing eighty-five percent free-throw accuracy rate, Dave was the only member of the Bulls who actually *enjoyed* going to the line at crunch time.

Dave, Chunky, MJ, Nate, and Jim were all on their feet. Nobody moved. Nobody talked.

Mark's first shot was up—and *good!*

The Bulls' guard took time between shots to defog his goggles—something he did at least ten times a game. Then he looked over at the Bulls' bench and, with a smile on his face, gave a thumbs-up.

Dave was amazed. *He's as cool as I would be out there! How could that be?*

Mark made his second free throw just as surely and calmly as he'd made the first.

The Bulls led, 52–51. Four seconds remained in the game.

The Panthers, with no time-outs left, scrambled to put the ball in play. Air Ball grabbed the inbounds pass from Duckworth. He raced upcourt and heaved a fifty-footer at the buzzer, but it fell way short of the basket.

"Bulls do it again! We're number one!" Chunky yelled as he and the rest of the Bulls' bench rushed out to swarm Mark, the hero.

"Indianapolis, here we come!" Brian chanted joyously.

But no one was more relieved than Dave. He just kept clapping Mark on the back, over and over and over again.

"Thanks, man," Dave said to Mark with a huge grin on his face. "I think you just saved my life."

Dave noticed Jim giving Mark a big bear hug. *Boy, did I ever luck out!* he thought. *Now Jim won't be able to blame me for an unnecessary loss. And after all this excitement, there's no way my mother can still be mad at me!*

CHAPTER 8

Mr. Bowman held two cans of cold soda in his hands.

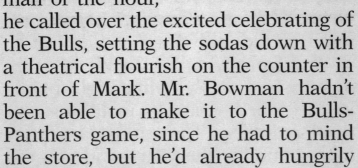

"We'll make that a double for the man of the hour," he called over the excited celebrating of the Bulls, setting the sodas down with a theatrical flourish on the counter in front of Mark. Mr. Bowman hadn't been able to make it to the Bulls-Panthers game, since he had to mind the store, but he'd already hungrily gobbled up all the details.

"Now, Mark," he continued, "don't lie to an old basketball player. Were your hands sweating *just a little* before those free throws?"

Mark swiveled around on his stool so that everyone at Bowman's could see and hear him. Dave could tell he was relishing his rare moment in the limelight.

"Wasn't worried at all, Mr. B.," Mark answered with a straight face. "I was as cool as the other side of the pillow. When you're a pro like I am, it doesn't matter if it's an empty gym at practice or a full house with a game on the line. A free throw's a free throw. You do what you gotta do."

Dave and Brian looked at each other, eyebrows raised, shaking their heads. "Gimme a break," Brian muttered, so that only Dave could hear.

"And from what I gather," the store owner went on, "you had eight points in the fourth quarter, including two three-pointers. That must be your high game for the year—and you did it all in six minutes!"

Dave had to admit that Mr. Bowman certainly knew how to make a kid feel good. *He realizes Mark doesn't love warming the bench—and now he's giving him the real hero treatment*, Dave thought. Mr. Bowman was, without a doubt, one of his favorite people in the world.

Mark continued to lap up the attention. "You're right, Mr. Bowman. My performance today should pretty much wrap up the Sixth Man Award for me. Goes to show what I could still be doing if Dime over here hadn't shown up to steal my starting spot!" he said, using Jo's nickname. Mark playfully took a backhand swipe and knocked Jo's ever-present green baseball cap to the floor.

Dave knew that Mark wasn't really upset with Jo. Mark was the team clown and didn't take anything too seriously. Besides, right from the start he'd been one of Jo's biggest supporters—even with his own starting job on the line.

Brian picked up Jo's hat and handed it back to her. "No, Mark, it's not Jo you ought to be replacing. It's Dave. We did just fine without him today." Brian gave Dave a wink.

"Nah," Will said, joining the assault. "We've got to keep Dave in the lineup so he can keep padding his league lead."

"League lead in what?" Chunky asked, playing the straight man.

"In technical fouls!" Will roared, pounding Dave on the back.

Everybody looked over at Dave to make sure he was taking the kidding all right. He smiled broadly, and everybody burst out laughing.

"Hey, you know what?" Dave said. "You guys can dis me all you want. I don't care." Then he raised his can of Pepsi as if making a toast. "Because we're going to the Final Four!" he cheered.

Brian raised his can high too. "I'll drink to that!"

"To Indianapolis!" MJ toasted.

"To March Madness!" Will added, thrusting his drink toward the ceiling. "To front-row seats!" Jo chimed in.

Dave lifted his can of Pepsi high with each toast, a satisfied grin plastered on his face.

In the midst of the celebrating, though, Dave saw Brian's smile freeze. Brian was facing the big storefront window of Bowman's. Dave turned to see what had caught Brian's attention.

Mrs. Danzig was at the window.

As his mother came in, Dave could see that her hands were shaking. Her face was set in an unfamiliar grim expression. He felt his heart speed up.

Mr. Bowman greeted her with a big "How you doing, Susan?" But Mrs. Danzig, who was usually extremely friendly and polite, didn't even respond. She looked straight at her son.

"David, I can't tell you how much you've let me down." She spoke softly, but the store had become so quiet that everyone could easily hear her. "You'd better enjoy this celebration," she continued solemnly, "because as soon as it's over, I want you home. And after today, you're grounded for a month."

Dave felt as though he'd been kicked in the stomach. In the excitement over the victory and clinching the March Madness trip to Indianapolis, Dave had forgotten all about his punishment. Or maybe he had convinced himself that his mother would let him off the hook.

"You can't say I didn't warn you," Mrs. Danzig added.

By now there was total silence in the store. Even Dave, master of the one-liner, was speechless.

Finally, with his mouth dry, he managed to ask, "A *month*? But that covers our next three league games. Plus . . ." He could barely even get the next words out. "Plus our trip to the NCAA finals!" he finally blurted.

His mother looked at him, her lips tightening. "Whose fault do you think this is? Mine?" she asked. "I'll wait for you outside. Good-bye, boys, Jo, Mr. Bowman." She turned and left the shop.

It was Brian who eventually broke the awkward silence that followed. "Don't sweat it, Dave," he said hopefully. "I know your mom. She's probably just bluffing."

"No," Dave said, shaking his head with conviction. "You don't know my mom like I know my mom. She was serious. *Dead* serious."

Again, silence.

Of all the things in the world that could happen to me, missing the Final Four trip would be the worst, Dave thought desperately. *Someway, somehow, I've got to find a way to make her change her mind!*

To be continued . . .

Don't miss Book #2 in the Super Hoops college championship miniseries: #11, **Above the Rim.** Coming soon!

After a twenty-second silence, Jim did address the players, but it wasn't with the fury Derek had anticipated. Actually, his voice was surprisingly quiet.

"Sure, you guys have won the March Madness contest," the coach said. "Congratulations. But you want to watch first place go down the tubes? Then just keep playing the way you played today."

Derek was waiting for him to say more, but Jim just grabbed his equipment and headed for the exit.

Nate shrugged. "I've got nothing to add."

As the Bulls slowly followed their coaches, Will mumbled to Derek, "Mark and Jo played a good game, but there's nobody like Dave at the point. I don't know what we're going to do without him."

Derek nodded. He'd come to the same conclusion himself. With Dave missing, the whole team was out of sync.

If we don't find a way to get Mrs. Danzig to lift Dave's grounding, Derek thought, *the Bulls are going to self-destruct!*

About the Author

Hank Herman is a writer and newspaper columnist who lives in Connecticut with his wife, Carol, and their three sons, Matt, Greg, and Robby.

His column, "The Home Team," appears in the *Westport News*. It's about kids, sports, and life in the suburbs.

Although Mr. Herman was formerly the editor in chief of *Health* magazine, he now writes mostly about sports. At one time, he was a tennis teacher, and he has also run the New York City Marathon. He coaches kids' basketball every winter and Little League baseball every spring.

He runs, bicycles, skis, kayaks, and plays tennis and basketball on a regular basis. Mr. Herman admits that he probably spends about as much time playing, coaching, and following sports as he does writing.

Of all sports, basketball is his favorite.